The Ghost Friend

Isabella Tesfaye

ISBN 978-1-63885-681-8 (Paperback)
ISBN 978-1-63885-682-5 (Digital)

Covenant Books
11661 Hwy 707
Murrells Inlet, SC 29576
www.covenantbooks.com

For my parents. Thank you for letting me experience my own adventures and solve my own mysteries.

Chapter 1

One light and not-so-stormy afternoon, Eliza B. Bettingworth was walking down the cold damp street, freezing to death. Only a short distance away from her home; you see, Eliza was known to overexaggerate. It wasn't even winter; it had just rained the day before. New York was her bright and beautiful home where she lived with her mother, Rachel, her father, Peter, and her nosy little brother, Charles.

Eliza's overexaggerations stemmed from the fact her family had just moved from London to New York. Eliza loved London—her friends Betty and James were the best. They would always play together and have the greatest time. While Eliza loved the bright lights of New York, she missed her friends back home.

The big city could be noisy, but at least it gave Eliza an excuse to stay up late. She especially loved Broadway and was thrilled her family was staying at an apartment nearby Times Square. The Bettingworth family moved because Eliza's dad got a new job as an assistant manager at a construction site of a new hospital. Eliza knew moving was for a worthy cause, but she wasn't happy to leave behind everything she'd ever known.

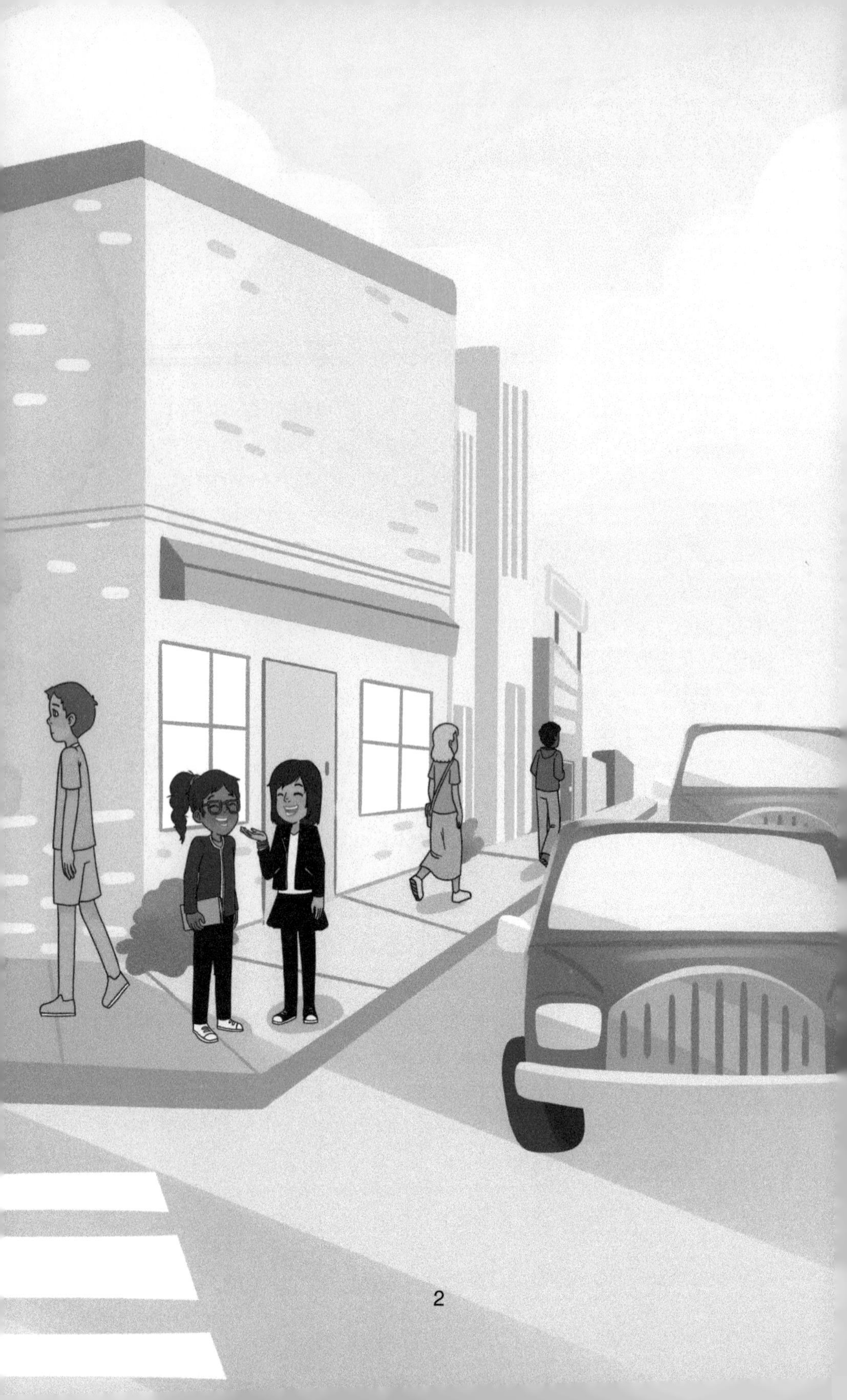

Eliza, now ten years old, went to a nice school called Astrid New Academy (ANA). But she didn't want to leave her wonderful life, home, and friends behind.

As she trudged down the sidewalk, Eliza spotted a girl about her age walking alone on the other side of the street. An opportunity to make a friend, Eliza walked over to say hello.

"Hello, my name's Eliza! What's your name?"

The girl replied, "Hi, Eliza! I'm Bethany Puseburt."

Eliza found out Bethany also went to ANA but had different classes. Bethany seemed really friendly, so Eliza decided to ask her to hang out.

"Do you think your parents would let us have a play date if you asked?"

"My parents don't live with us," said Bethany. "I live with my grandma. My mom and dad disappeared when I was young."

Eliza knew she shouldn't ask any more, but she was definitely interested. She made a mental note to investigate. Back home in London, Eliza was the greatest detective in town, like a mini-Nancy Drew!

When the girls finally arrived at Eliza's apartment, it seemed as if they'd been walking for hours. Eliza walked inside, and when she turned around to say goodbye to Bethany, she was gone! *How strange*, she thought. When Eliza got to her room, her mom greeted her with a kiss.

"Hey, hunny, how was your day?" asked Rachel, who looked beautiful as always. Rachel had beautiful dark brown curls that stopped at her chin.

Unsure how to reply, Eliza said, "Intriguing, Mom. It was interesting."

Just then, Eliza's nosy little brother, Charles (or Zippity Chuck, as Eliza called him), burst into the room screaming, "Mom! Mom! Eliza met a little weird girl, and the little weird girl ran!"

Now Rachel was interested. "Honey, what's going on?" she asked Eliza.

Eliza couldn't believe it! Charles was being such a— well, such a Charles! Eliza began thinking of spells to make Charles pay.

Charles, Charles, you're such a pain.
Charles, Charles, you shall be slain.
I'll turn you into a frog if it's the last thing I do.
I'll make you pay and you'll go boo-hoo.

Eliza knew it wasn't nice, but she was so mad she could just spit. To top it all off, Mom would not stop bombarding Eliza with questions. Eliza didn't know what to do.

She said, "Charles, you're such a pain! And, Mom, Bethany is my friend. I thought you wanted me to make friends so there. And yes, she did run off." Eliza finished by saying, "CHARLES, YOU'RE SO ANNOYING!"

Charles started crying. Even though he was five years old, he acted like *such* a baby sometimes. Eliza was unhappy and was exhausted from her walk home.

Tomorrow was Saturday, so she decided to get a good night's rest so she could do some investigating in the morning.

Chapter 2

The second that Eliza woke up, she greeted the day by grabbing some cereal out of the cupboard before diving into some investigations. Upon hearing some commotion outside, Eliza looked out the window to find Bethany walking down the street by herself. But before Eliza could sum up her thoughts, Bethany had disappeared.

Hmm.

Eliza opened her laptop to see what she could dig up. Her family would wake soon, and she still hadn't found anything on Bethany.

Weird.

Eliza decided she would search Bethany herself. After carefully typing in "Bethany Puseburt," she found an image of an older woman. Well, that couldn't be right. Bethany was only ten years old.

Eliza's mom was awake now, making pancakes for Charles. Eliza asked if she could go down to the docks to see the water. Being extremely protective, Eliza's mom said yes, but only if Mrs. Micknerfy accompanied her.

Mrs. Micknerfy was not only a nanny to the Bettingworth kids, but also the most *boring* person ever. She'd never let the kids do anything, and to top it off, she snored like *crazy* (and she slept right next to Eliza). But Eliza was determined to figure out this mystery, so she said yes. Eliza and Mrs. Micknerfy went down to the docks in the early afternoon. Surprisingly, she found Bethany there by herself, dangling her feet over the water.

Eliza also saw an old fisherman with a lot of fish. Eliza went to talk to him and asked him if he knew anything about an older woman named Bethany Puseburt.

The man gasped. "H-how do you know that name? Never say it again!" said the old fisherman in a thick Irish accent.

Eliza wondered, *What was so bad about the name?* So being the curious kid she was, she asked the man, "What's so bad about the name Betha—" Before she could finish, she cut herself off, remembering what the man had just said. "What's so bad about…the name?" She corrected herself.

The man had been smiling when Eliza went over to him initially, but now he had a rather serious, perplexed look on his face.

"Little girl," he started, "that name has not been heard since my time, which is a *long* time ago. Oh, my name is Mr. Luchicha, by the way. But let's get back to the story."

Eliza was intrigued, listening intently.

"Okay," Mr. Luchicha continued, "that name—not just the first name, but the whole name—was said to be cursed. There was an old lady who actually lived next to me, and she was the person who had that name. She was said to be a witch, and one day, she mysteriously disappeared and was never seen again. Now people say if you run into anyone with that name, it has to be a ghost because that name wasn't heard of again once people started complaining to officers. So never repeat that name again because it will bring misfortune and you will—"

The man stopped after seeing the scared look on Eliza's face. But Eliza was curious now and was desperate to know more. The man wasn't in the mood to continue the tale. So Eliza left and didn't ask anymore. By the time the fisherman was done, Bethany had once again disappeared.

A storm was starting to roll in and, by the time Eliza and her nanny returned to the house, the wind was rapidly blowing. Eliza picked her laptop back up but couldn't find any little girl who went by the name of Bethany Puseburt.

Eliza decided she was going to talk to Bethany, and she couldn't sleep at all that night. She was so worried something was going to go wrong. It was already weird seeing Bethany at the docks and her disappearing, along with the old man's tale.

The clues didn't add up.

The next morning, the sun seemed darker and the day felt gloomy and humid. Eliza's every step to school felt heavy and dangerous.

How would Bethany react? What would she say? Would misfortune fall upon Eliza for asking?

After what seemed like *forever*, the bell rang, and Ms. Crangmire's class was finally over. Eliza found Bethany walking down the usual sidewalk and, before Eliza could take another step, Bethany spotted her and turned behind her.

Eliza felt doomed as she walked up to Bethany and said, "How are you, Bethany? Um... I have a question." Eliza was feeling hesitant and heavy, asking the question *way* louder than she wanted to.

"Bethany, what is going on?" she continued. "First you disappear out of thin air, and then I talk to a man at the docks who said your name wasn't heard of again, and unless your parents just wanted to stir up trouble, then sure, be named that. But also, this creepy old lady was named that and…um…you're not a creepy old lady, right?"

Once Eliza stopped talking, Bethany's face was filled with anger. Eliza could tell Bethany wanted to run her over with a bull.

Bethany, her face red as a tomato, said, "Seriously? You went and searched me on the internet and followed me to the docks and took information about my name from a *creepy old dude*? I can't believe you would do that! What is wrong with you?" If Bethany wasn't already filled with anger, she sure was now. She turned around rapidly and sped off. Eliza stood there in shock because she didn't get any information and because Bethany, her only friend, just took off! Eliza walked back to the apartment alone and found her mom on a work call for dinner while Charles was picking his boogers—so gross.

Eliza carried her backpack to her room, replaying the conversation in her head. Wait, how did Bethany know Eliza had looked her up online? She hadn't mentioned that. *Weird.* Now Eliza's brother was banging on her door for maybe the fifth time today.

"Yes, Charles, what do you need for the fifth time!" Eliza yelled.

Charles answered, equally as loud, "Well, Miss Meany Pants, Mom is calling you for dinner, and also, you are the meanest!"

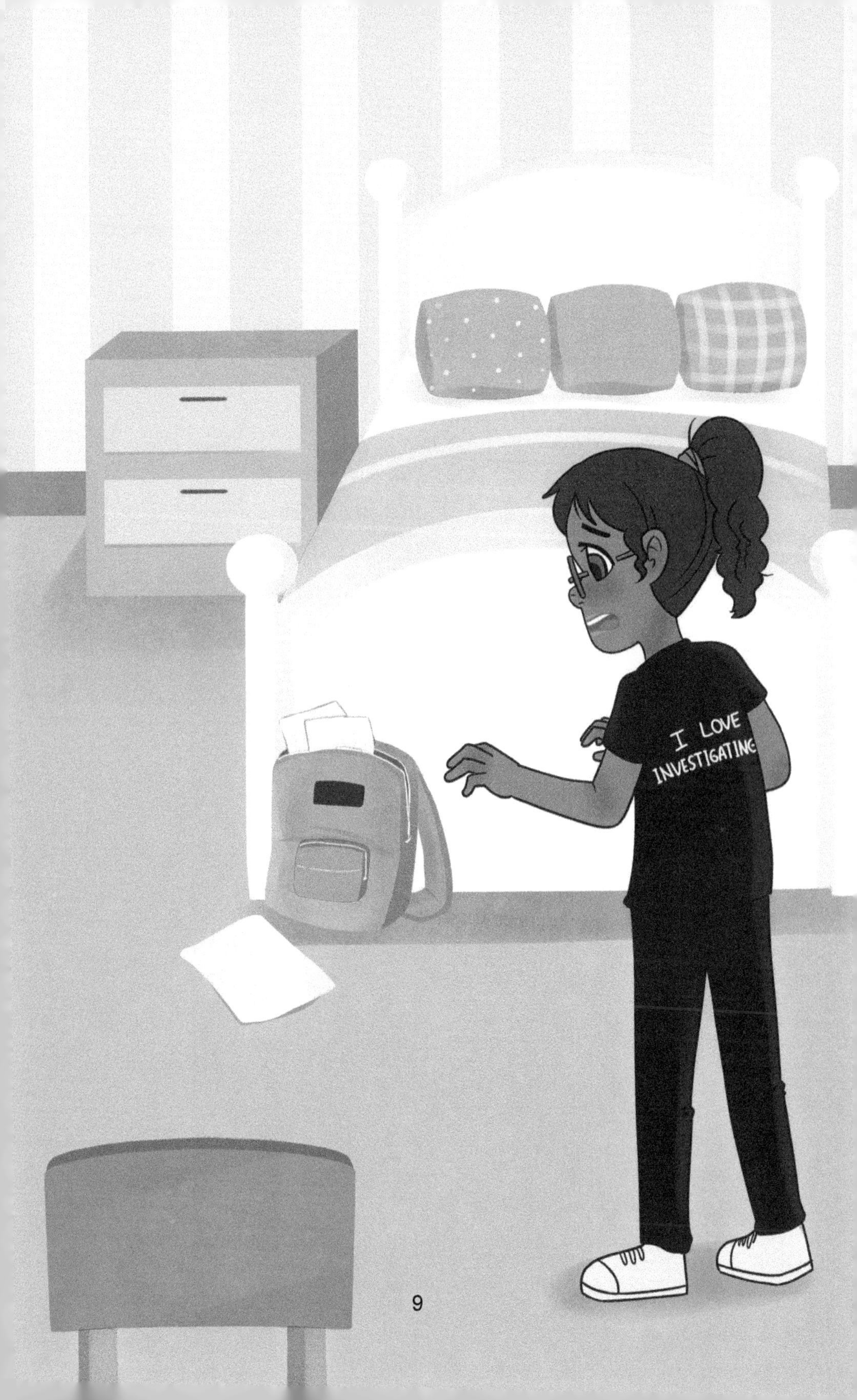
I LOVE
INVESTIGATING

Eliza was hungry, so she opened the door and walked to the kitchen for dinner, ignoring Charles who was being a pain in the butt and yelling, "Eliza, you are so mean! You didn't even say thank you! And I'm the person who told you that dinner was ready."

Eliza sat down, and her mom asked her about her day.

"Mom, my day was okay," said Eliza, knowing this wasn't a satisfactory answer because her mom loved to know *everything*.

"Well, why wasn't your day spectacular?" asked Rachel.

"Because I had English and Math and everything else," said Eliza. Now her mom was firing questions at her faster than she could answer.

"What did you do in Math and everything else that was so boring? Did you make any new friends?"

Eliza had zoned out now, thinking about her earlier conversation with Bethany. How did she know she looked her up? Eliza was about to go to her bedroom when the doorbell rang. Eliza answered to find it was her dad. She and her brother greeted him with big bear hugs and kisses. Rarely did he come home early!

Eliza went to retrieve a test she'd gotten an A-plus on to show her dad when something suddenly flew in her window. It was a piece of paper. Eliza gasped with shock and horror, dramatically throwing the paper on her bedroom floor. The note had said:

You know too much; watch your back. I know what you know, so stop investigating or suffer the consequences…

Eliza's dad was calling her now. She stuffed the paper into her investigation binder and rushed out the door.

Chapter 3

Eliza had fallen asleep on the couch that night, so her dad carried her to her room. Eliza woke up and went downstairs for breakfast. Mrs. Micknerfy was already up making cereal for Eliza and pancakes for Charles. When Eliza finished her breakfast, she went upstairs to get ready. When she got upstairs, she put on her jeans and her "I love investigating" T-shirt she had gotten at the spy museum with her mom and friends.

Eliza took the note out of her binder and read it again. She wondered who would give this note to her; it could be anyone, but Bethany was her number one suspect. Bethany knew about the online search, and she made a big scene; Eliza might've deserved that, but who else would send her a note like this? Bethany was the only person she had told about investigating. Eliza's mom was now calling her to come downstairs. She stuffed the mysterious paper in her binder and dashed out the door.

Eliza was walking to school when she saw a familiar man—it was the man from the docks! Eliza followed him. He seemed to be heading to her dad's construction site. When he arrived, he turned around, and Eliza ducked. As the man was going in, he dropped something and ran into the site. Eliza went to pick up the piece of paper. Yet another note, but this one had a special printing on the bottom with two strange numbers. It said:

I thought one note would be enough, but here's number two. Stop following me. I know you. I can hunt you down, and after you follow me a third time, your daddy's construction site's going down.

Eliza gasped. *Who would want to hurt her dad?* Then she noticed the numbers on the bottom: 7-2-77990 and 22-9178-003. What could they mean? They appeared to be handwritten.

Eliza pulled out her investigation binder. She opened her secret compartment to retrieve her magnifying glass. She studied the note carefully and didn't find a thing until she looked at the upper left-hand corner to find a logo that appeared to be cut up. It looked like it said "I-S-R-A." Eliza had seen that logo before. It was the ice-skating rink's logo! She took ice-skating lessons there three times a month.

Eliza was about to head to the ice-skating rink when she looked at her watch. Yikes, it was already 8:10 A.M., and her class would start in five minutes! Eliza couldn't be late for class, so she ran as fast as she could. She stopped at her locker for her textbook when she saw Ms. Crangmire. Eliza received a tardy slip and went to class. Eliza sat down when she noticed something on the floor. Thankfully, it wasn't another note but a weird drawing of a ghost by the docks. It could be helpful, so she tucked it into her investigation binder.

When Eliza got out of school, she headed for the skating rink. Observing the lockers, Eliza looked back at the note and realized the first number on the note was also the first number of the locker. Eliza scanned the area for locker seven. After finding it, she put the combination in and opened the locker to find a bunch of supplies. She then noticed a little compartment at the bottom that was locked. Eliza thought about breaking into it but feared getting into trouble. Then she remembered the other handwritten numbers on the note.

She unfolded the note and put the numbers in. She slowly opened the compartment and fell back at the horrifying sight.

Chapter 4

It was a picture of a ghost. It looked very strange, as if it was wailing. It looked so real—like Eliza could be transported in time just by touching it. It looked as though the lady was calling out her name.

Eliza… Eliza… Eliza.

Eliza put her hand on the drawing and touched the lady's face. Suddenly, her hand went through the paper, and she could feel someone grabbing her hand, pulling her, and calling out her name, louder now.

Eliza… Eliza… Eliza!

Meaner and louder, the sound came closer and closer as Eliza tried pulling back out of the grasp. Suddenly, she heard something behind her and, when she turned, the lady's grasp let go. A tall man with red hair and a goofy face was standing behind her. His name tag read Dan Girohst.

He stared at her with a blank expression before saying, "Are you okay, young lady? You look as though you've seen a ghost!" Looking at Eliza more closely now, he said, "You don't look so good."

Eliza, stunned into a temporary silence, finally said, "I'm okay, sir, thank you. But I have to know whose locker this is."

With that, the man grew suspicious. "It's Mr. Luchicha B.'s locker," he said quite quietly.

Eliza turned around for a second and thought about the picture. Then she turned back, and the man was gone.

Eliza took the drawing, stuffed it in her bag, and walked up to the check-in table. She asked the man at the table if he had seen Dan Girohst leave. The man looked confused.

"There's no one here by that name," he said.

This man might be important, Eliza thought. Asking for a pen and paper at the desk, Eliza quickly wrote down the name and left the ice-skating rink. As she looked up, the sky seemed darker now—ghostly, in fact.

Eliza was in her bedroom thinking about what happened that day. *Why would the man from the docks have a picture of a ghost woman, especially a scary living one?* Eliza thought about it. Was she going crazy thinking a photo could literally pull her in?

She took the paper out of her backpack, careful not to touch it. It seemed though that the picture was calling her again as if it wanted her to jump in. *Eliza… Eliza… Eliza.*

She heard her name being called again. As she looked closer into the photo, she saw something. She couldn't quite make out what it was, so she leaned in closer and closer until something grabbed her by the same arm. Now it was holding her nose, and it was getting hard to breathe. Eliza pulled and pulled until the hand finally let go but, as the hand let go, something dropped off of it. It was a bracelet with several charms on it: a ghost, a treasure box, a skull, and a strange key in the middle.

Eliza wondered what the key was for or what it opened. Perhaps a door to a secret passage or a treasure chest! Eliza gasped. A treasure chest!

That's what she spotted in the photo. Pulling everything out of her backpack, something fell out. It was the photo she had picked up in school. Eliza stared at the picture. The ghost in it looked surprisingly like the ghost from the other picture; except this one had her head down, and there was another person in the background. Eliza looked closer at the picture, sure that this one wouldn't grab her.

She looked closer when suddenly the lady's head shot up. The lady had a sad expression at first but then she looked angry and mad as if she wanted to kill Eliza. She floated closer and closer until she looked like she would jump out of the page. She looked as if she was trying to get out of the picture, and she banged on the page.

Eliza couldn't take it anymore! She flipped the paper around and saw something. Handwritten words in big bold letters that said:

PROPERTY OF BETHANY PUSEBURT
DO NOT TOUCH

Why hadn't Eliza seen that before? It was right there. While Eliza was thinking about it, the ink faded away. Eliza had so much to figure out: the picture, the ink, and—oh gosh, Eliza had just remembered—Dan! Dan Girohst; perhaps he could be connected? Eliza studied his name for minutes before she got bored. She then took out her invisible ink and scribbled over the words.

She noticed some of the letters in his name stood out. The G, the O, the H, the S, and lastly, the T. Eliza gasped and switched around some of the letters. They spelled *ghost*. This didn't make any sense.

First Mr. Luchicha B. tells her about the old lady, then she finds a picture that comes to life, then everything happened with Bethany, and now Bethany's picture came to life—oh, and now Mr. Dan Girohst. Or should she say, Dan Ghost! Why *ghost* though? This didn't make any sense.

Eliza sat in her bedroom, confused. She was staring at the bracelet again when there was a rapid banging on her window. Actually, the banging sound was everywhere. Eliza turned this way and that, and all around her there were ghosts. Tons of them—screeching, reaching, and trying to touch her.

Eliza was now breathing rapidly. They couldn't touch her though; it was like she had a force field surrounding her. She looked down at the bracelet to find that it was glowing. Eliza's head was turning and spinning. She then heard an ear-piercing scream. She looked up at a ghost that looked like Bethany.

And that's when Eliza fainted.

Chapter 5

Eliza woke up dazed and confused.

What had just happened? It all went by so fast, and Eliza couldn't remember anything other than the room was shaking. Maybe it had just been a normal earthquake.

Eliza went downstairs and asked her mom if there had been any notice or any happenings of earthquakes. Eliza's mom replied with a shake of her head. No earthquakes.

Eliza went back to her room to figure out what was happening. She tried to remember *anything*, but she just couldn't.

She decided to sleep and attempt to figure everything out the next day.

Eliza woke up and looked down at her wrist because it was hurting her. Then she noticed she had slept with the bracelet on. Eliza changed out of her pajamas and went downstairs for breakfast.

Her mom was making eggs. Rachel turned around, looking relieved that her daughter was awake. Rachel mentioned Eliza's dad had forgotten his lunch, and she was heading to work so Eliza offered to bring it to him. She ran upstairs and put on her sneakers before rushing back downstairs to grab her dad's lunch.

Eliza was walking down the street when she bumped into someone. She looked up and let out a gasp, leaping back a little.

It was Mr. Luchicha B. His face had a blank expression which soon morphed into one of hate. Eliza started running backward, but Mr. Luchicha B. was following her.

"You know what you did," he said. "You will pay."

Then the footsteps behind her stopped. Eliza turned around, and Mr. Luchicha B. was gone. Eliza was terrified. She didn't know what would happen next. She thought back to her last encounter with Mr. Luchicha B.

It had been at her dad's construction site.

The letter. *Oh no.*

Eliza ran to her dad's construction site. She got there in time. Nothing had happened. That's when she walked in and noticed her dad pacing around.

"What's wrong, Dad?" she asked.

He told her one of the wooden beams had caught fire and the job was now off course by eight days. Eliza felt so bad. She knew it was her fault that her dad's hard work had gone down the drain. Eliza felt like everything was her fault. She didn't know what to do. She gave her dad his lunch and left.

Eliza returned home feeling horrible. She went to her bedroom and cried. She took out the picture from her binder again—the one that belonged to MRB. She looked at it, feeling anger toward everyone. She ripped the paper into a million little pieces.

Then something started talking to her.

It said, "Eliza, you shouldn't have done that."

The picture put itself back together, one piece at a time. Eliza was in shock. Then all of a sudden, some force pushed her closer and closer to the picture. She put her feet down trying to stop the force, but she was too late.

The picture had swallowed her whole.

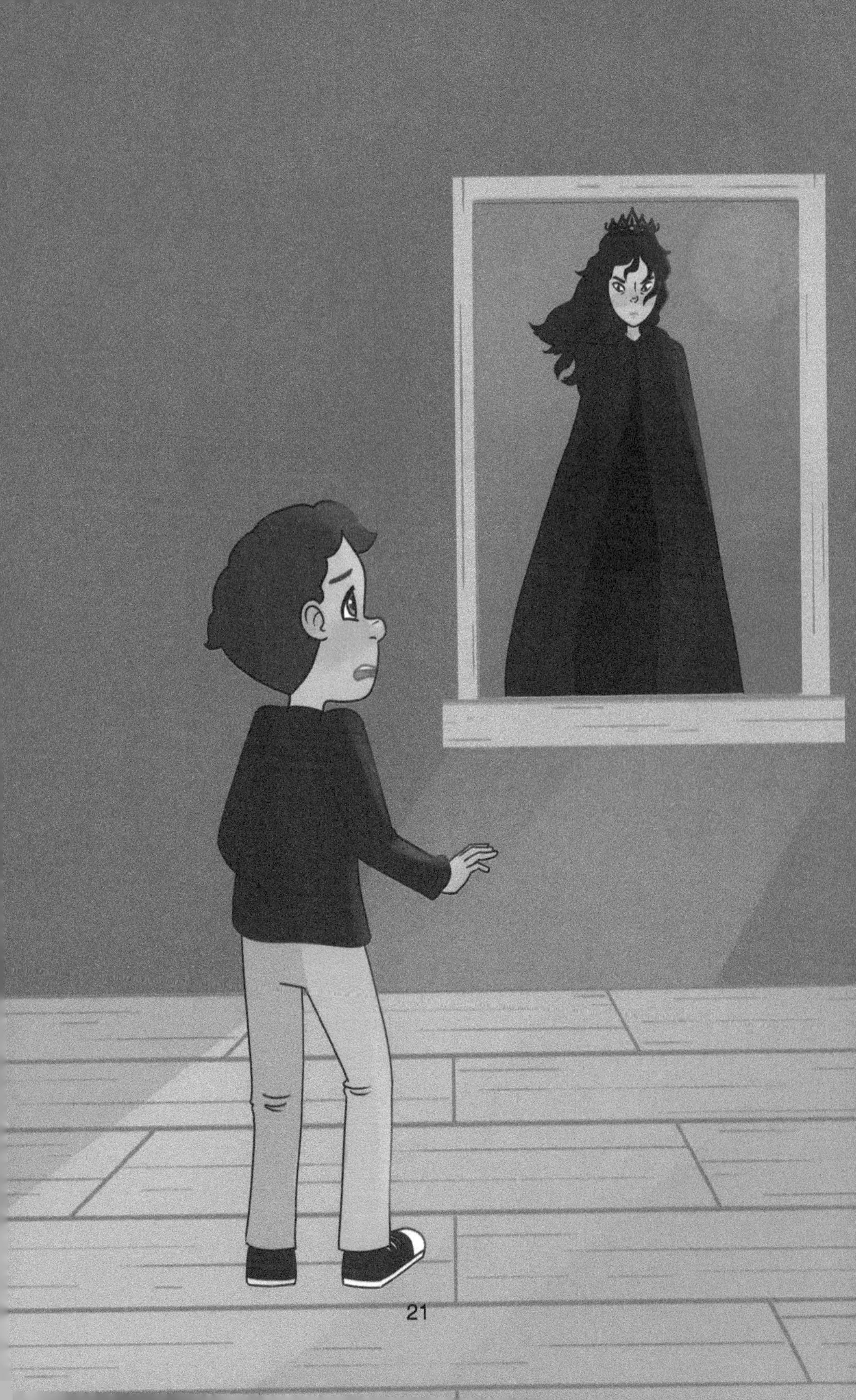

Chapter 6

Eliza observed her new surroundings. It looked like she was in the middle of a village. Someone was hunched over her—a boy who was about her age. Eliza looked around and noticed everyone was a ghost while this boy appeared to be human. Eliza poked at his face.

"Ow," the boy said in what sounded like an unusual accent.

"Sorry," Eliza said. "Just checking if you were a ghost, but you appear to be human."

The boy told her he was human. Eliza had a million questions, but she decided to start with the three most important ones.

"What is your name? How old are you? And how did you end up here?" she asked.

He told her his name was Luke, he was eleven years old, and it was a *long* story how he got there. He told her she could come with him to his home and tell her. Eliza was hesitant at first; he *was* a stranger after all. But she had nowhere else to go. So she followed without question.

After a short walk, Luke told Eliza to stop; but when she looked around, she saw no house. Luke put his hand on what looked like thin air to Eliza, but it was a wall to him. When he put his hand on the wall, a house showed up. Like magic! Luke ushered Eliza inside, and she looked around. It looked like a regular house. Eliza saw a round table with some chairs and sat down. Luke joined her and started talking.

"So I was awake in my bedroom thinking about ghosts," he started. "I had a nightmare about them and couldn't go to sleep. Then when I was going to close my eyes, a pair of green eyes started staring directly at me. I didn't know what to do, so I talked and asked the lady, 'What are you doing in my bedroom?' She told me she could make my dreams come true. At that time, I lived with my uncle, and he was very cross and sometimes mean, and he would draw the most unusual drawings."

Eliza stopped him right there. "Who is your uncle?" she asked.

"His name is James, the second Luchicha B.," Luke said.

Eliza got up from her chair and started to slowly pace back and forth.

"What is your name?" Luke asked Eliza. "Can I tell you something?" he said after learning her name. "It's important."

Eliza was hesitant but finally said yes. Then she followed Luke upstairs into a small quiet room. Luke asked her to sit. He looked worried and afraid.

"Let's start off from where I left in the story." Luke started. "I wanted to go with the lady. She was beautiful, and my uncle was mean, and that's when I went to my uncle's room to tell him what had happened. I saw a glowing light in the tiny doorway. I opened the door a little bit and heard my uncle say a few words: 'Need to open the door… ghost.'"

Then all of a sudden there was a loud noise outside and the ground shook with the thunder of footsteps.

Eliza looked out the window, but Luke didn't have to.

He knew what it was, and it wasn't all that good.

Eliza asked Luke what was going on. She could see people marching down the street. Eliza saw their faces. They didn't look happy, and she wondered why. Luke said there was a queen of this town called Queen Marabella. She was not nice. Luke told Eliza the queen had been watching her. All the pictures Eliza had seen had been of her. Luke then told her the queen had recently lost her bracelet and had been angrily searching all over town for it.

With a worried expression, Luke added, "Eliza, I have been watching you from this world. I know what happened, and from all I've seen, you should hide. I saw the queen's bracelet when she was pulling you in. And I saw it slip off. That bracelet gives her magical powers, but if it's on anyone else, then it protects them."

Luke stopped, and Eliza almost fell backwards. She had so many questions; she didn't know where to begin. Unfortunately, Eliza would have to ask later.

Eliza heard the door bang open and, before she could ask who it was, Luke shoved her into a closet and shushed her. Eliza heard a whooshing sound and saw something fly by in a blur. It had to be the queen—she had loads of jewelry on and a long black dress.

She had a stern face that looked like she'd never be happy ever again. Eliza heard the queen ask Luke, "Have you seen any odd people in the village?"

Luke replied with a shake of his head. "No, Your Majesty, I have not."

Somehow the queen saw through him because she added, "Are you sure? Because if you lie to me, there will be—" She stopped as if unaware what to say. "Let's just say there will be serious consequences," she ended.

The queen shot a look directly toward the closet Eliza was in. Then she stormed off into the sky. Eliza came out of hiding. She was scared because she knew the queen was not happy with her. She had to find a way to get out of this weird ghost world. After a few moments of silence, Eliza asked Luke a question.

"Luke," she started, "is there any possible way I could get out of here? This ghost world that trapped us?"

Luke was silent for a few minutes before he walked to the window. "I've been trying to escape forever," he said. "It's difficult to escape this world. I have tried many, many times and have failed. But we could try together."

Eliza was excited now. She wanted to know how to escape the horrible world. Eliza was the most eager she'd ever been in her life. She asked Luke what they had to do to go.

Luke's face seemed worrisome, but he answered, "First we have to get the stick from the three ghost witches that live on top of Mount Ghostiny, which is a hard task for humans. Second, we need to take a piece of the old glass jar in the museum, which is heavily guarded. Then the hardest task: we need to get the queen's bracelet from her."

Eliza didn't know about the first two, but the last one seemed easy.

"Well, we already have the queen's bracelet!" she exclaimed, lifting her wrist.

But she was shocked to find it was gone.

Eliza looked at Luke, but he didn't look as shocked.

"I don't know how, but I think the queen took it back," he said.

Chapter 7

Eliza felt as if everything was being drained out of her.

How was she going to get home back to her mom and dad and Charles? How was she going to escape this horrible world? These tasks seemed to be getting harder by the moment.

When Eliza looked up, Luke was staring at her.

"Why are you looking at me funny?" Eliza snapped. "Don't you see I'm not in a good mood?"

But that's when she realized her skin was glowing blue then red then blue again. Eliza screamed and jumped up: that's when her skin turned normal again. She stared at Luke for a moment then asked him why this happened. He always looked normal and calm but now he looked even more shocked then Eliza.

"I don't know," he said.

Eliza didn't want to spend another minute in this horrible world. Without another word, Eliza grabbed Luke's hand, and they dashed out the door.

It was cold and dreary outside, but Eliza knew they would have to fight through it to get out. She didn't know the first place to go.

"Where is Mount Ghostiny?" Eliza asked Luke.

"I don't…know…sorry."

Eliza was bursting with anger and she wanted to go home. But if Luke didn't know where to start, she'd have to figure it out herself. She asked him where the nearest map store was and, after he didn't reply the first time, Eliza asked again, a little louder than she had meant.

Luke replied, unsure but quickly, "Go straight, then turn, then…turn…again."

Eliza was so frustrated, but she said calmly, "Please, can you just show me if you can?"

Luke and Eliza were walking when they came upon the perfect store for this situation: Maps and Stuff. Luke opened the door to the eerie store. It was all dark except the tiny light peeking out the window. Someone creeped behind Eliza and said, "Boo!"

Eliza screamed and turned around, but it was just a little ghost boy.

Eliza peered closer at the ghost boy and he appeared to be laughing very hard.

"Ahh, I got you so hard, scaredy-cat! I can't believe the way you jumped. Hahaha!"

Eliza was not in the mood for an attitude like this, so she marched to the boy and made a speech. "Mister, I am not in the mood for this kind of behavior. I would like you to please show us where the maps are right this instant, young man. Now fix yourself up and get moving. Stop being rude."

The boy looked shocked as if nobody had ever spoken to him so sternly before. Eliza was wondering why he wasn't moving and why he looked so scared.

"Why do you look so frightened?" she asked him. "I only spoke to you sternly. Has nobody ever spoken to you like this?"

The boy didn't answer and, before Eliza could say another word, Luke stopped her.

"No, I'm afraid no one has ever spoken to him like that," said Luke. "He's seven years old and was transported to the ghost world just two years ago. His parents had never had the chance to speak to him in a stern manner. He was quite a good kid, and here in the ghost world, he doesn't have anyone looking out for him except—" Luke stopped midsentence when a ginormous shadow stood behind him.

It was the shopkeeper, Mr. James Porter.

"Me, you were going to say. Yes, I keep this boy out of trouble whenever I can. Well, I only accomplish that duty sometimes. This boy gets himself in lots of trouble, I'm afraid. What trouble is this?"

Eliza was staring at the giant man. She knew it was rude to stare but she couldn't help it—he was a giant! There wasn't any man this tall and big in London or New York. When the man looked at her, she stopped.

Luke replied to the man first, "Nothing, Mr. Porter. But can you show us where the maps to…um… Mount Ghostiny are?"

Mr. Porter replied, "Mount Ghostiny! Why would you ever want to go to such a wretched place?"

Even though the man knew Mount Ghostiny wasn't the best place to go, he retrieved the map for them anyway.

Eliza and Luke thanked him and dashed out to start their adventure.

Chapter 8

Eliza and Luke had been walking for hours. Eliza was so tired and worn out. But they had to keep going if they wanted to survive. It was hard though because everywhere they went people would stare at Eliza.

She asked Luke why nobody was staring at him; they were both human after all. Luke told her he had disguised himself when he came.

Suddenly somebody stepped in front of them and said, "Hello, what is a human doing in the streets of the ghost world, hmm?"

Eliza was about to tell the boy when Luke stopped her.

"Nothing," he replied to the boy.

Eliza and Luke kept walking when the boy called out to them, "I can help you reach Mount Ghostiny."

This time, Luke stopped walking. "Who are you, and how do you know where we're going?" he asked the boy.

The boy replied, "Thanks for asking. My name's Jack, and my friends heard you talking about your mission to get out. I can help you. I'm actually friends with the three witches. But I'll only help you if you promise to let me get out of this world with you."

Luke looked doubtful. "You're dead. You can't come out of the ghost world."

Jack told them to follow him. Luke didn't want to at first, but Eliza convinced him that he might help them. So they followed him. He led them to an alleyway.

"I'm actually human," Jack said as he pulled off his face. Eliza was horrified but soon realized it was just a mask.

"Lorenzo," Luke said, "what are you doing here? How did you get here?"

"I was there that night when you saw the lady," said Lorenzo. "She came to my room too, and she told me to come with her, and then she sucked me into a portal. I'm assuming she did the same with you because you're here."

Eliza was very confused now. "Luke, who is this?"

He replied, "My brother, Lorenzo."

Eliza just stared at them blankly as they talked. She was assuming she'd have to put the pieces together by herself because they weren't going to finish talking any time soon. So she assumed that the lady took Lorenzo and Luke from their uncle's house and brought them here, but she was tired of listening, and night was falling upon them. So she told them to get a move on, and the trio were on their way once again.

The trio found an inn where they decided to rest for the night. While they were walking, Eliza was thinking of how the queen had stolen her bracelet and, if she had, why she hadn't taken Eliza too. Possibly even killed Eliza if she was a threat.

Eliza was in her own little world, dazed, when she bumped into a petite little old woman. Eliza was really sorry, so she apologized to the woman. Then she looked around and realized Lorenzo and Luke were gone; she must have stopped following them when she started thinking.

She looked back at the old woman. She appeared to have lost something, and Eliza wanted to find Lorenzo and Luke, but this old lady needed her help, and she knew they would look for her as soon as they realized she was gone. So she went to the old lady and asked her what she had lost.

"Little girl, I've lost my spectacles, and I can't find my way home," the lady said. Eliza felt bad, so she helped the lady to her feet. And they were on their way to the old lady's home.

They stopped in a little old alleyway. The lady looked at Eliza with a sly grin. Eliza was getting scared. So she asked the lady what was going on when a big puff of smoke came out of nowhere. Eliza screamed when she saw who was staring at her from the smoke. It was the queen. Eliza was then tied to a chair so fast she didn't know what was going on. She was petrified—she couldn't die! She couldn't become part of the ghost world yet. Not without seeing her family and her friends.

"Please don't hurt me or kill me," Eliza screamed.

"Kill you! I would never do that," she heard.

Eliza was so relieved. She breathed out all the air she had been holding in.

"Because then where would that get me? I'm going to use you to open up so many doors for me. I'm not only going to be ruler of this world but of your world too," the queen said.

"How would you do that?" asked Eliza. "Why do you need me?"

The queen replied, "Because you are a part of the other world, and I need a person from the other world to get in. I can't do it by myself and plus, you're…special."

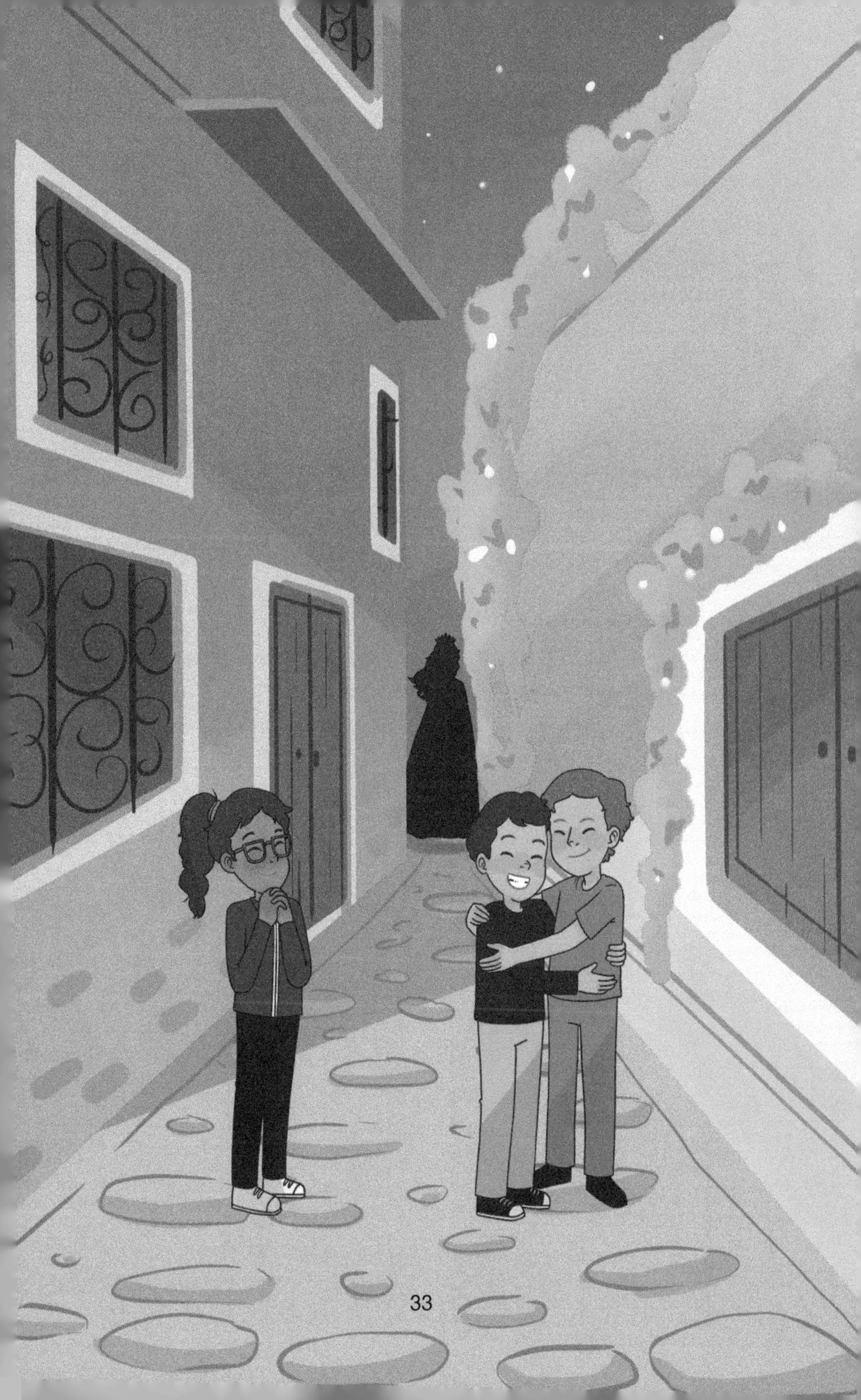

Eliza was confused that the queen had gone out to pull her, Luke, and Lorenzo in. Why couldn't she do it on her own?

Eliza asked, "You pulled me in, and didn't you have to enter my world to do it?"

The little old woman standing by the queen's side was about to tie Eliza up in a bag when a shadow flew over them. A shadow oddly shaped like two boys. Eliza didn't have to see anymore; she knew Luke and Lorenzo had come to her rescue. It was all a blur, but she saw a few puffs of smoke and then all of a sudden she was free and she wasn't tied up anymore.

She heard Lorenzo call out to her, "Run!"

She was running like she had never ran before. But then something big shadowed over her like a giant mountain. Then they knew they had reached Mount Ghostiny.

Chapter 9

Eliza was so happy she didn't even think about how steep the mountain was; she started climbing right away. But she lost her balance after the first four steps. She asked Luke and Lorenzo why she couldn't climb, and they said because it wasn't really a task that could be achieved by humans. Luke and Lorenzo could go because when they had disguised themselves as ghosts it had given them the powers to float. But then that meant Eliza couldn't go with them and she would have to stay behind.

Luke and Lorenzo had reached the top where they could finally see the witches' hut. Luke had remembered what Lorenzo had said earlier about how he was friends with the witches.

"Okay, Lorenzo. Go tell them to give us the stick."

Lorenzo seemed confused "Why me?"

"Because you're friends with the witches," Luke said.

Lorenzo had just remembered what he had said. "Oh that," said Lorenzo. "I made that up so you guys would take me with you."

Luke was slightly annoyed but he got over it. They went and knocked on the hut door. The witches didn't answer, so Luke opened the door himself. The witches weren't happy with the rude barge in.

"What do you want, you little child?"

The oldest one said her name was Exima. She had no hair and wrinkled skin and a big wart on her nose; she wore her witch's hat and only had one eye. The second one, Hagel, wasn't any better looking. She was short and she had a hunch back and crackly skin, a disfigured nose, and messy gray hair.

"I don't like kids! Get them out of here," Hagel said.

And lastly there was the youngest and prettiest witch named Agnes. She was a witch in training and was tall with short blond hair, no warts, and a smile that glowed when her sisters weren't looking.

"I think we should ask them what they want first," said Agnes. Hagel and Exima were not happy with their sister's niceness.

"Ugh, why are you so nice? You're supposed to be a witch," Hagel and Exima said.

Agnes wanted to tell them there were good witches and she wanted to be one, but she knew that would result in fighting, and she didn't want to fight.

"So, children, what do you want?" Agnes asked.

Luke and Lorenzo didn't know how to say they wanted the stick, because they knew the witches wouldn't give it to them because it was the magical stick that they used to give them their powers. Exima represented the sky, Hagel represented the earth, and Agnes represented the people—meaning she could read their minds and tell them what to do.

"We would like the stick please," said Luke.

Hagel and Exima burst out laughing. Nobody expected this.

"You think we're going to give you the stick?" Hagel said

"Wow, we were wrong about kids. They're hilarious," said Exima.

"No, we're serious," Lorenzo said with a very serious face. "We need the stick."

"Wait, you're serious? No! Are you kids crazy? I would never, in a million years, give you the stick," said Exima.

"Please. What would you like? We'll give you *anything* you want just please give us the stick," Luke pleaded.

This time Agnes spoke up which nobody was expecting. "There is something we want, but it's harder to get than anything."

"No, Agnes, we don't want anything. We won't give the stick," said Exima.

But Agnes didn't even seem to notice.

"We want you to give us the Cauldron of Fire," she said.

Everyone gasped. This was something nobody had ever gotten in a million years.

The Cauldron of Fire was a cauldron that granted the person who beheld it three wishes, but it's severely guarded by a dragon that's said to never sleep and only feasts on those who are foolish enough to enter his cave.

This was going to be harder than they thought.

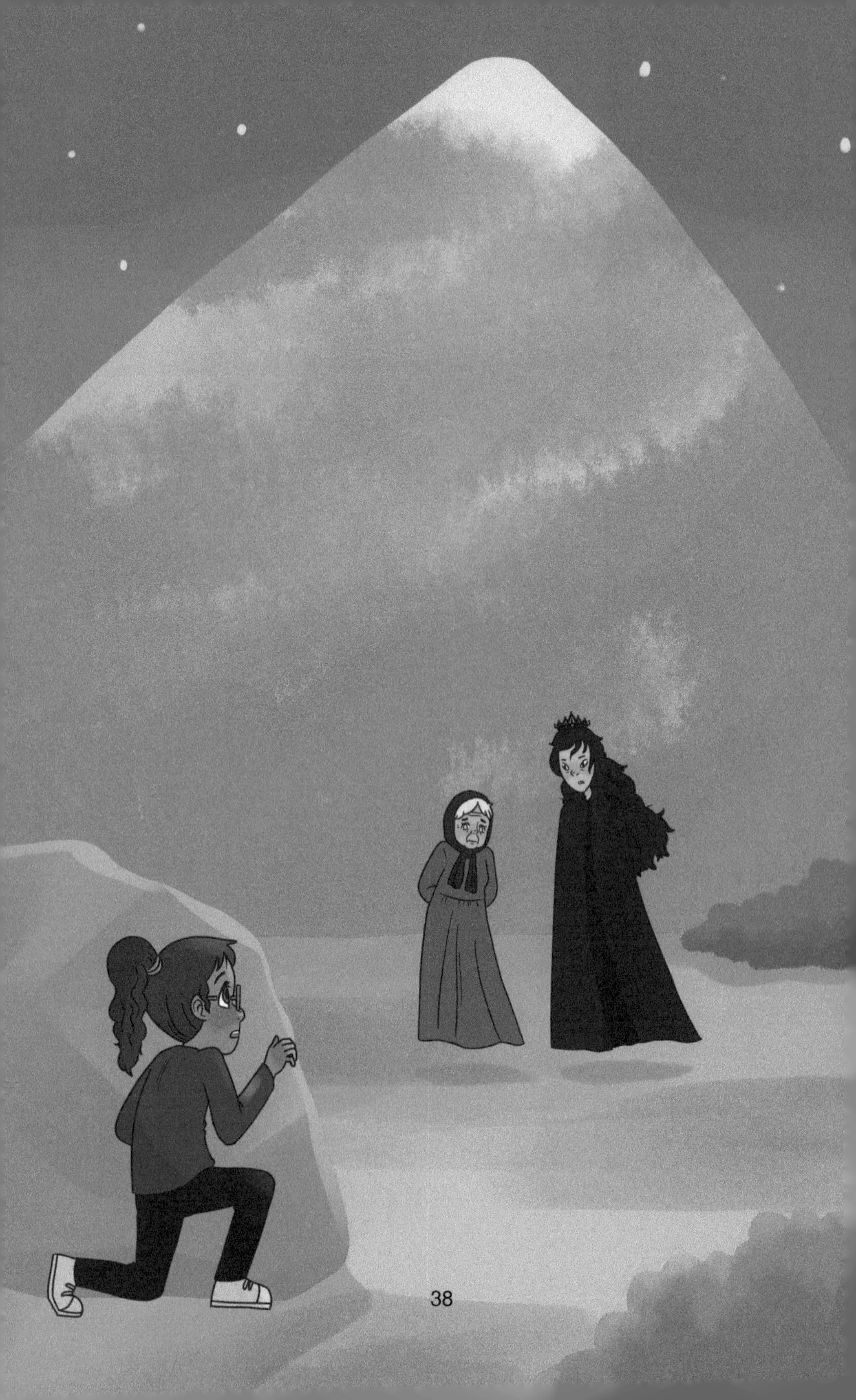

Chapter 10

Eliza waited for the boys at the bottom of the mountain. So far nothing had gone wrong. Eliza was watching the people pass by; everyone looked so busy as if they all had somewhere important to be. It reminded her of New York. Suddenly, out of the corner of her eye, Eliza spotted the queen. Luckily, she had not seen Eliza though she was headed her way. Eliza quickly hid behind a rock, but unfortunately, the queen decided to rest at that very rock.

Eliza overheard the queen talking to the little old lady.

"I want that girl," said the queen. "She's the only way I can get into the other world."

"With all due respect," replied the little old lady, "why can't you do it yourself? You *did* transport to the other world to get all those kids."

"Because," the queen continued, "I had to use a very strong burst of magic to get in there for just a few minutes. But if I transfer the magic that's inside of her back to me, I'll have all the magic I need."

"My queen," said the little old lady, "that girl has no magic in her! She's just like any other human girl."

"No, Eliza comes from a magical family. Her great-grandparents were magical. We need to go, come on."

Eliza was in shock as she came out of hiding. Not only were there more kids to save, but she was from a magical family herself!

Eliza and the boys met at the bottom of Mount Ghostiny. Eliza was bursting at the seams after hearing what the queen said.

"Guys! Guys!" shouted Eliza. "I saw the queen, and she was talking to this little old lady, and they said there were *more* children that the queen had teleported. And she said she needed me to get into our world because when she tried to trap more children, she ran out of magic. But she also said I'm magical. Apparently, my great-grandparents were magical!"

When she finished her speech, the boys looked shocked.

"So you're magical? And there's a bunch of other kids scattered around this place?" Lorenzo said.

"Yes, that's exactly what I'm saying!" Eliza replied.

"Well, we went to the witches' hut," said Luke. "And they agreed to give us the stick, but only if we could give them the Cauldron of Fire."

They would now have to go get the Cauldron of Fire, which would set them back about three days. It was going to be dangerous because they didn't know how to get there. But the trio decided to continue on.

Eliza, Lorenzo, and Luke each had a lot on their minds. Eliza was thinking about how she could potentially use her powers to save the other kids. Luke was thinking about how they were going to pass the dragon to get to the Cauldron of Fire. And Lorenzo was thinking how Eliza might be able to use her powers to summon a fake Cauldron of Fire for the witches.

"Eliza," said Lorenzo, "what if you could use your magic to make a fake cauldron?"

Eliza has magic, but she'd never used her powers before.

"I'm not sure I'd know how to do that," she said.

Lorenzo had another idea. Eliza could learn magic at Ugga's Magic Spot. Ugga was a greedy ghost who loved money. They'd need at least two coins to enter and five more for magic lessons. When Lorenzo shared this idea with the others, they decided to go for it.

Chapter 11

At Ugga's Magic Place, things were not going well. Ugga's son had tragically been transported to the afterlife. Because of this, the queen decided to pay a visit to Ugga to express her condolences. Walking around the tight, cramped space, the queen was disgusted. Earlier in the day, the queen had spotted Eliza, Luke, and Lorenzo. She knew of their plot to visit Ugga.

"Oh, dearest Ugga," said the queen, "I'm so sorry for your loss. We just can't stop crying. I think I know how your son died."

In shock, Ugga vowed to make whomever hurt her family pay.

"I was walking to check on my wonderful citizens," said the queen, "when I overheard a few children talking. Their names are Eliza, Luke, and Lorenzo. They were talking about killing your son—your wonderful son who has done nothing but give back to our community. I'm so sorry I didn't make it to you in time."

The queen even managed to cry a few fake tears for Ugga's sake. The queen knew Ugga was easily angered; however, she needed to really drive the point home. She decided to put a spell on Ugga, with what little magic she had which immediately turned her heart to stone.

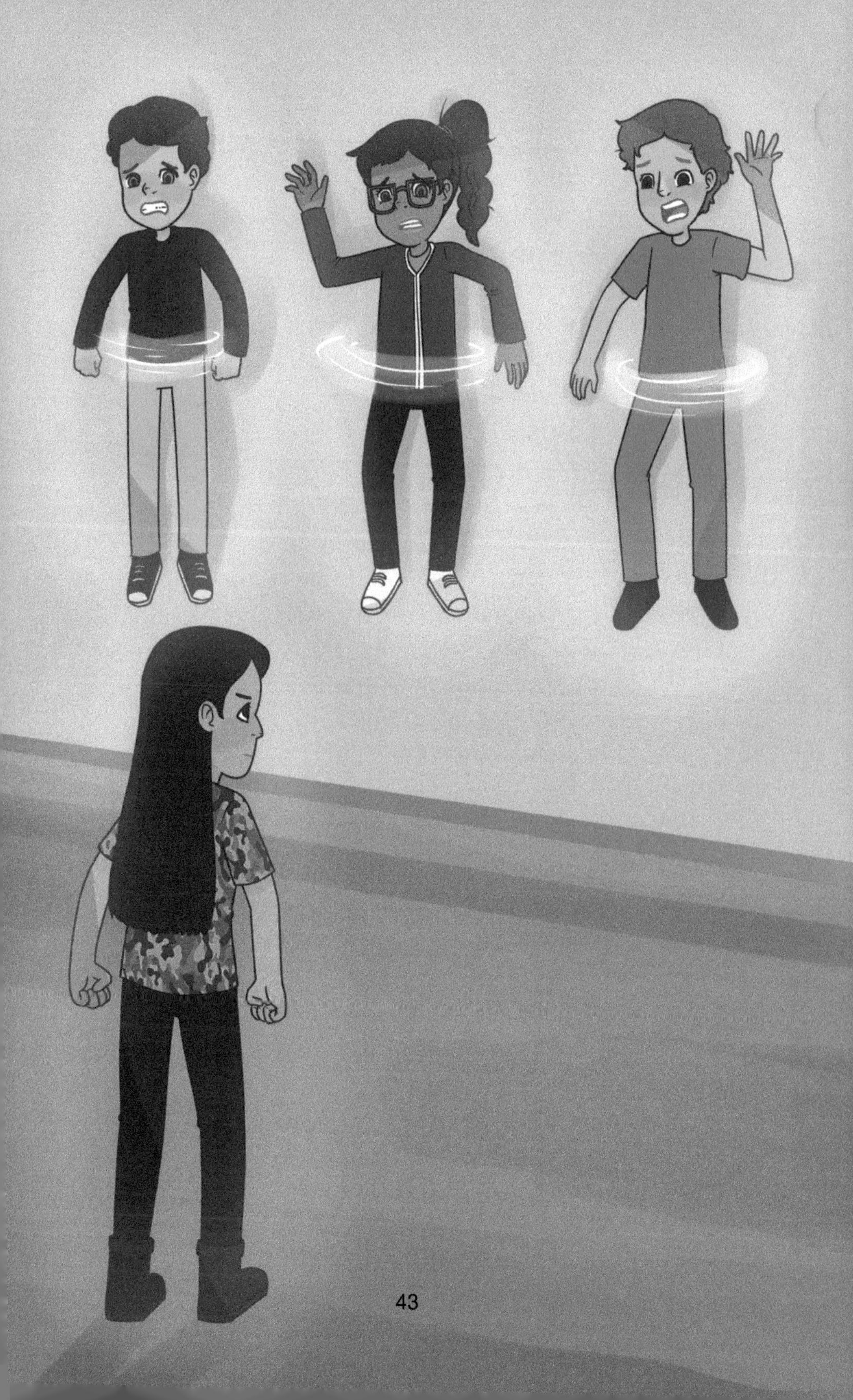

Before leaving, the queen made a point to remind Ugga of the children's names.

"Don't you forget them," she said to Ugga.

The trio were on their way, having fun and cracking jokes with one another. Once they arrived at Ugga's store, they walked inside to find Ugga staring blankly at the floor. Upon seeing the children, Ugga's eyes started to glow and her face turned pale as her hair became white. Suddenly, Ugga was floating—becoming a monster of the queen's creating!

"Who are you?" Ugga shouted in a deep, scary voice. "Were you welcomed? I think not!"

Finally, Lorenzo mustered up the confidence to reply. "Sorry, ma'am," he started, "my name is Lorenzo, and this is Eliza and Luke. We were hoping to receive magic lessons."

Ugga couldn't take it. She screamed, and the children were suddenly pinned to the wall.

"What do you want?" Eliza asked on the verge of tears. "Please don't hurt us, please!"

Ugga nearly laughed at this.

"I want to know why you've hurt me," she replied to Eliza. "Why have you hurt my family and my son?" Ugga's eyes were filled with anger.

"What?" Eliza was confused. "We don't know what you're talking about! We would never hurt anyone."

Ugga's inner voice fueled her hatred. *They're lying to you. Don't believe a word they say.*

Ugga screamed. "I will not believe your lies!"

The voice returned. *Get the girl. She's the main leader.* Ugga reached out for Eliza when there was a sudden *boom!*

A tall black-haired girl appeared out of the blue. She wore army boots, black pants, and a patterned top.

"Cover your noses," the mysterious girl told the trio.

She then sprayed the room with a toxic chemical which made Ugga collapse to the ground. Once Ugga was down, the girl released the children from being pinned against the wall.

"What's your name?" Luke quickly asked.

"My name's Victoria," she replied. "But everyone calls me Vickie."

"Are you a ghost?" asked Lorenzo. "You have legs, and ghosts don't have legs."

Smiling, Vickie laughed and said, "No, I'm not a ghost. I'm completely human."

Before she could continue, Eliza had to ask the most important question: "How did you get here?"

"Well," started Vickie, "I don't remember much. I was walking, and all of a sudden everyone around me froze in place. Then I saw a lady walking towards me with her hand held out. She had on a long black dress and tons of jewelry. She told me to come with her, that I would be the happiest person alive if I did. But I said no because my dad was frozen, and I didn't want to leave him. She didn't care and pulled me in anyway."

Eliza knew exactly what happened. "Of course," she said. "You're another one of the queen's victims. The queen traps children and takes them here."

Vickie understood this but was still unclear on something else. "Why doesn't she trap adults?" she asked Eliza.

"I—well—I don't really know why," Eliza said.

Ugga was going to wake up soon, so the trio had to leave quickly. They started to head out without a second thought.

"Hey!" Vickie shouted from behind. "Where do you think you're going?"

"We're trying to get out of this world!" Lorenzo yelled back. "And we're going to get the Cauldron of Fire. Eliza was going to make one, but she doesn't know how to use her magic."

"Okay, wait!" said Vickie. "Can I come with you? I have some experience with magic and might be able to help."

The kids were thrilled and, without hesitation, told Vickie to come along. They soon found a safe house to spend time practicing magic together.

Soon Vickie helped Eliza to make a perfect replica of the Cauldron of Fire.

Chapter 12

With the perfect replica of the Cauldron of Fire in tow, the team pushed onward and left a very confused Ugga back at her store. The group soon reached Mount Ghostiny. Lorenzo and Luke started making their way up the mountain while Eliza and Vickie stayed at the base.

Luke found the witches at home and put his ear to their door. He could hear Exima and Hagel yelling at Agnes for telling the boys that they could have the stick. And now they were unable to break this promise to the boys because even though they were witches, they always kept their word. This was because one time long ago, one of their ancestors broke a very important promise and it caused her to become cursed.

The boys decided to burst in through the door announcing that they had the Cauldron of Fire. Exima took the cauldron as Hagel handed them the stick. Exima didn't know what to wish for which bought the boys time.

They ran down the hill as fast as they could as they heard Hagel scream loudly, "They broke their promise!"

Now the crew had one item down and two more to go if they wanted to return home.

Vickie led the way as the group continued on to the National Museum. Eliza was about to go in when Luke stopped her in her tracks.

"Remember," Luke said, "this place is heavily guarded. They're watching our every move, and there are cameras everywhere. But don't worry, I've got these."

Luke pulled out four walkie-talkies.

"When did you get these?" Eliza asked. She had been with him this entire time and never noticed the walkie-talkies.

"I pack them every time I go out of the house," Luke said, "just in case I need them! Good thing I had four."

With their walkie-talkies in hand, they went inside. Eliza bumped into something and landed on her bottom. She looked up to see a large man.

"Sorry, ma'am," he apologized. His voice boomed, reminding Eliza of Santa, minus the cheery tone.

Standing up, Eliza brushed herself off. "It's okay," she said. "I wasn't watching where I was going anyways."

"What are you kids doing here?" the man asked. Turns out, he was one of the guards.

"We're here because we wanted to look at the museum," said Vickie. "We hope to see all the wonderful artifacts here."

"Well then don't let me stop you," said the guard. "Go right ahead."

The four of them took a brochure and a map from the front desk and decided to split up. No one knew exactly where the old glass jar was.

Eliza started to walk through the history exhibit in awe of all that she was seeing. She'd never known the ghost world had such a rich history. Soon she came across a door that said in big bold letters:

Do Not Enter
Government Business

Eliza, ignoring the sign, walked in and found an exhibit on the various queens. Queen Marabella was described as a ruthful queen with a troubled past. Apparently, her mother died when she was young, but she didn't let that get in the way of her dreams. Her mother had always wanted to be queen, so the girl decided to fulfill that lifelong goal for her.

In that moment, Eliza felt pity for the queen. But then she noticed a note at the bottom that said, "Queen Marabella, 1963–2016. May she rest in peace. Reporter: Old Lady Smith."

Eliza reread this over and over again.

It was 2017. If the queen had died in 2016, who was this other queen?

Meanwhile, Luke had found the old glass jar and was running to find the others when he bumped into one of the security guards. This guard was rather unforgiving and told all of the children to leave, never to return again.

"Yikes!" said Vickie, her face long with sorrow. "I guess we have to start from scratch."

Eliza was distraught. "I don't know what to do. We need to get out of this ghost world though. Is there any other way?"

Eliza couldn't help but think of her parents and how worried they must be. Luke and Lorenzo and Vickie were hard at work, scanning their brains for useful information.

Finally, Lorenzo shouted, "There is a way!" He continued on, "Just as in the human world, security guards take shifts so they don't have to work around the clock. We still have a chance! I remember what the guard looked like."

Overjoyed, Eliza was beaming with happiness. But she soon remembered what she had seen in the museum regarding Queen Marabella. Her face turned somber.

"What's wrong, Eliza?" Vickie asked, sensing trouble by the look on her face.

Eliza recounted what she had learned; now the group of kids were unsure and nervous.

It had been more than half an hour as the group sat outside the museum's entrance in silence. The sun had fallen behind the trees, adding to the gloomy feel of the day.

Suddenly, a tall uniformed man left the museum, and Lorenzo recalled that this was the guard who kicked him out. Standing up, Lorenzo started to make his way inside.

"Where are you going?" Luke asked his brother.

"I'm going to get what we came here for," Lorenzo replied. "That was the guard; it's safe for us to go in now!"

The team split up again, each taking on different routes this time. Vickie was the first to come across the old glass jar. She knew she couldn't just run out with it, so she stuffed it into her backpack—forgetting about the security cameras! She used her walkie-talkie to let the others know to meet her at the entrance. The original trio met her there, excited to leave, when one of the guards grabbed Vickie's backpack.

"Ma'am, I need to check your backpack before you leave," he said.

The others were so nervous and scared as he began to search her pack. Vickie, on the other hand, looked as cool as a cucumber.

"Sir, do you know who I am?" she said to the guard.

The guard took a step back, shocked at this rude remark. "Young lady, do you know who I am?" he retorted. "I am a very highly-respected officer, and I will not let you speak to me like that."

Vickie scoffed. "As I was saying before you rudely interrupted me, I was the president's daughter in the other world."

Eliza, Luke, and Lorenzo couldn't believe their ears. They continued watching Vickie and the guard go back and forth.

"You think that means anything here?" the guard said to Vickie. "She's not in this world, so it doesn't matter."

A grin spread across Vickie's face. "Listen," she said, "when my mother gets into this world and the queen passes into the afterlife, who do you think will be the queen here?"

The guard didn't back down. "How do you know she will become the queen?"

Vickie's grin became even wider. The team did not understand what she was doing!

"My mother," continued Vickie, "is not only the president of the other world. She is the daughter of the queen of the ghost world."

The guard's face changed dramatically.

He bowed down to Vickie and said, "Oh…umm… well, my queen—my princess…um… I mean—yes, you can pass."

And so off the team went.

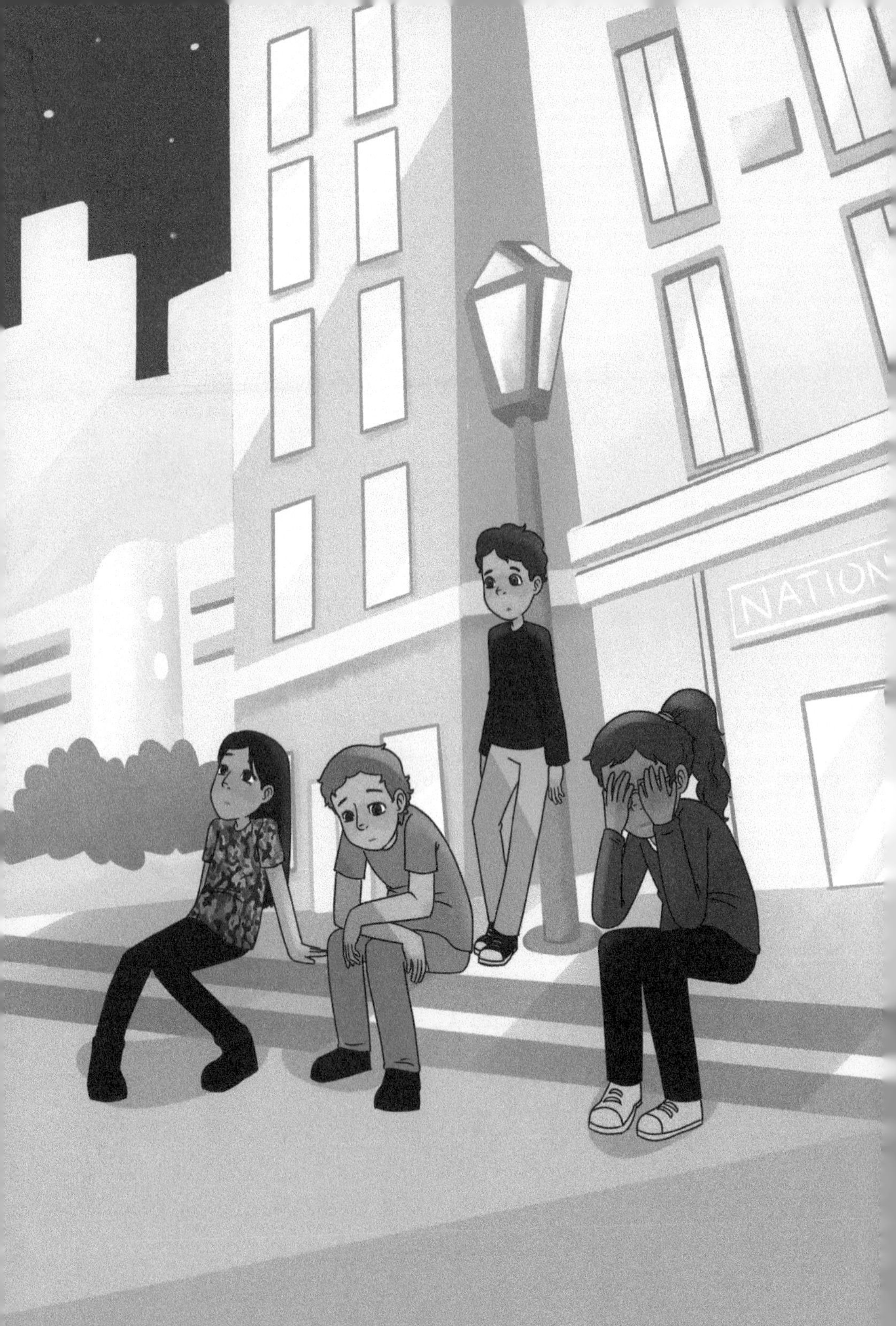

The team walked out of the museum, avoiding any further suspicion. The rest of the group had been quiet as Vickie continued laughing. Finally, Eliza couldn't take it anymore.

"Why didn't you tell us you were the president's daughter?" Eliza yelled. "And that she is the daughter of the queen of this world! Queen Marabella. Queen MA-RA-BE-LLA!"

Vickie only started to laugh harder which made Eliza more confused.

"Why are you laughing?" Eliza asked.

"My mother isn't the president!" said Vickie. "She was a lawyer. But I had to come up with a way for the guard to let us through! I just can't believe he fell for it. He may be the highest-ranking guard, but he's definitely not the sharpest."

At that, Luke started giggling and then Lorenzo burst into a laughing fit; finally, Eliza joined in, and soon, they were all sitting and laughing on the curb.

As night came upon them, the group found a local inn to stay in. They discussed their next steps.

"What do we do about the queen?" asked Lorenzo. "You know she died and went to the ghost world after the human world. But now she's in the afterlife. I don't understand why there's no new queen."

"Yeah," agreed Luke, "why is someone posing as the queen? Why can't she say her real name and show her real face?"

"And why didn't they want anyone to know?" asked Vickie. "Someone was bound to go into that room at the museum and find out."

Everyone turned to look at Eliza who had yet to say anything.

"Sorry, guys," she said. "I was just thinking. If Old Lady Smith was the reporter—well, if she's still here, maybe we can go talk to her."

Vickie agreed with this idea as she'd been thinking it too. "Sounds good!" she said. "But first let's get a good night's sleep and some food too! I'm starving." Vickie was thinking of the idea in her head.

Suddenly Eliza was confused. "Wait," she said, "you can *eat* in the ghost world?"

"Well yeah," said Vickie. "They still need food, or else they go to the afterlife. They just have an extra layer of ectoplasm so you can't *see* the food."

"What's so bad about going to the afterlife?" Luke asked.

"Oh, it's not all that great," said Vickie. "There's a ruler there. I know, we have a lot of kings and queens, and you never pass once you're there. You just stay forever. And the King has been in rule since…well…forever, and he makes the citizens work as his slaves.

Luke asked, "How do you pass on to the afterlife?"

"The same way you pass into the ghost world," said Lorenzo. "You stay here for a certain amount of time and then *poof*, you're gone! Oh, and however old you were in the human world is the age you are in the ghost world."

"Yeah," said Vickie. "I came here not too long ago, only a couple months."

Eliza was curious to know exactly how old Vickie was?

"Well, it's only been a couple of months, and when I came here, it was 1993," said Vickie.

The whole team shouted, "What!" in unison.

Luke was the first to say anything. "Vickie, it's 2017. You're thirty-four!"

Vickie's face went pale. How could she be old? She hadn't aged a bit!

The team was stunned into silence and didn't talk the rest of the night. When morning came, they'd have to start their journey anew with several more mysteries to crack.

Chapter 13

Morning was creeping in, ray by ray. It looked to be a delightfully sunny day, but the team felt more confused and dreary than ever.

"I have an idea," said Eliza. "What if we ask Old Lady Smith about the queen? And we ask one of those really wise old people about Vickie?"

"That's actually a really good idea," Lorenzo agreed. The team agreed, and off they went to find Old Lady Smith.

They were walking and looking in the streets for someone wise when they came upon an alleyway.

Eliza stopped.

"Guys, come here," she said.

The team hurried her way.

"Look! There's an old lady sitting over there," said Eliza. "Maybe she can help us."

The team nodded in agreement, and they all rushed down the alleyway. The lady was looking down so none of them could see her face, but she was wearing rags and a tattered blanket.

"Um, excuse me, ma'am. We would like to ask you a question, and we think you have the answer."

The woman still didn't talk.

"Um, ma'am—guys, I don't think she's going to talk."

Suddenly, the woman's head slowly rose and she didn't have a face—only a mouth! The group jumped back against the wall. The lady started forming words with her mouth, the only part of her face, and then it started to pour rain and thunderstorm around them. At first no one could understand what the woman was saying, but then they could see it appeared she was asking for help.

Vickie started crying. "I know what's happening I—come on, let's go to the library."

The team didn't know what to think, but they wanted answers, so they followed Vickie. Once they got to the library, Eliza burst out all the questions that were filling her mind.

"Vickie, what's wrong?" she asked. "Are you hurt? Did that woman do something to you?"

Vickie replied, "It wasn't her. I'm Old Lady Smith. That was the queen. Well, the *old* queen. Her spirit is still here, I guess. I promised the bad new queen that I would help you guys and steal information for her."

"You—you betrayed us!" Eliza shrieked. "What do you benefit from helping her and from betraying your friends? Well, I guess we're not your friends because we don't even know you!"

"You guys *are* my friends," promised Vickie. "The queen said I wouldn't go into the afterlife if I worked for her. She…she's very powerful. You don't know what she's going to do to you, and she's watching us right now, and she told me that if I told you I… I would go there, so—" Vickie wasn't crying when she said the last word of her sentence.

"Wait, so you're leaving?" asked Lorenzo.

"Are you going to the afterlife?" asked Luke.

Eliza just remained silent, thinking of what the queen would do to them and to Vickie. Vickie had been silent too, and her last words to them were not happy ones.

"The queen, she's going to—" Vickie started to say. All of a sudden, there were blue speckles all around, and Vickie started to fade away. Her last words were, "I'm sorry. Goodbye!"

"She never got to tell us what was going to happen. She…she never even got to stay long," said Eliza.

Lorenzo was mad. "She betrayed us!" he shouted. "How can you be sad right now? I'm… I'm furious!"

"You guys," said Luke, "we don't know what the queen is going to do to us. I don't think it's a good idea for us to go and look for the queen's bracelet anymore."

What would happen next? they all wondered in silence.

Chapter 14

As the team pondered what to do next, Eliza felt a sudden wave of anger toward Luke.

"It's easy for you to say," she mumbled under her breath.

"What was that?" Luke said.

"Oh, nothing," Eliza replied. "It's easy for you to say that we can just quit."

Luke was shocked. Eliza, normally so polite, was being *so* rude.

Eliza continued, "You don't have a family waiting for you back there or, at least, not a very good one anyway."

"That's...that's absurd! You...that's..." Luke was struggling to find the words.

"See?" said Eliza. "You don't even know what to say, and you know why? Because I'm right."

"Both of you please stop it!" said Lorenzo. "You're both wrong. We all have family back home waiting for us. This is the work of the queen. She's doing something!"

"Well then," said Luke, "we should get a move on."

"Yes, we should," said Eliza, eager to be right and answer before Luke.

So the team became the trio once again. The queen's palace was a long walk from where they were, and they were in need of a break. They went to a local restaurant called Judy's Café. Lorenzo was Judy's friend.

"Judy's very old," said Lorenzo. "I believe it's her twenty-fifth year in business. Everyone's been here. Judy is the owner, and she used to run this cafe with her daughter. But her daughter ran off, but everyone still comes here because many of the other stores are shutting down."

"That's odd," said Eliza. "Why are they closing down?"

Luke knew the answer and replied before Lorenzo could. "Most of them were new businesses and small businesses such as coffee shops and other cafés. A lot of people wanted something new, a change, so they went there. But suddenly all the people started coming to Judy's, and the other places went out of business."

"That's odd that they just got up and left the new places to go to an old place that they'd already been to," remarked Eliza. "Strange, don't you think?"

Just as the boys were going to say something, their waiter came to take their orders.

"Can I get you anything to drink, folks?" asked the man in a suspicious voice.

Eliza was busy looking down at her menu.

When she looked up to say she wanted apple cider, she was no longer looking at the waiter but at the mysterious Dan Girhost.

Eliza jumped back in her chair. "Do I know you? You're Dan Girhost!" she exclaimed.

Dan was grinning as if he was a fox about to catch his prey.

"That is what it says on the name tag, ma'am," he replied. "Now what would you like to drink? An ice-skating rink shake, a ghost-picture juice, or would you like a 'Luchicha B.'?"

The boys weren't listening as they were too busy trying to decide on soda or lemonade. Dan smiled his evil smile again. Luke decided on soda while Lorenzo asked for Lemonade.

"Guys," said Eliza. "something weird is going on. Can we go? Please? I'll tell you later."

Just when they were going to get up, Judy came over looking flustered.

"I'm so glad you're here," Judy said. "I need your help! Come with me."

The trio got up and followed her into the kitchen where they found the most unpleasant surprise in the world—the queen.

Standing next to the queen was Dan; the old lady from before, Judy; and Mr. Luchicha B.

The trio had a bunch of questions. Eliza had her suspicions about Dan, recently Judy, and Mr. B, and she'd always known the old lady that had kidnapped them in the beginning of their journey was evil. But Eliza never thought they would work for the cruelest mind in the ghost world.

"Long time no see, Eliza and Luke and Lorenzo. You've been here for a few months. I thought you would have perished by now." *A few months!* Eliza thought.

The evil crew the queen had created laughed—all except Mr. B.

"What's going on?" Luke asked.

"Yes, Uncle, we want answers" Lorenzo said.

"I'll tell you what's going on, children," the queen answered. "All these people are dead, of course."

The trio had a lot of questions and were all confused, but the queen didn't give them time to ask their questions.

The queen continued, "Yet you've seen them in your world. I've sent them to your world. They work for me because I've promised that as long as they stay loyal to me, they won't go to the afterlife. What they do in your world is they open portals for me. But I need children's power to do that, and so I take children from your world, and I suck up all the power and energy in them. But I don't normally get *all* the power I need. Once the portal is fully opened, I can stay in the other world for as long as I want. And I am going to rule your world. Once I do that, I'll look for other galaxies in the universe and I'm going to rule those too."

The queen delivered this news with the most evil look the kids had ever seen.

"That wasn't smart," Eliza said.

"What was that, dear?" the queen said through clenched teeth.

"It wasn't very smart telling us your plan," said Eliza.

The queen let out a smile again. "You think you'll be able to do anything or tell anyone where you're going?"

At that very moment, the queen opened a portal, and the tragedy and horror of the afterlife flashed right before their very eyes.

The trio was sent deep into the heart of the afterlife.

About the Author

Isabella Tesfaye was born in Fairfax, Virginia. She loves writing, and has competed in various essay and poem contests. She now lives in Lorton, Virginia, with her parents and two siblings—one sister and one brother (his name isn't Charles, though). This is her first book.

CPSIA information can be obtained
at www.ICGtesting.com
Printed in the USA
LVHW071744190422
716634LV00025B/1047

9 781638 856818